I0817381

Careers in Artificial Intelligence

Joshua Gregory

Published in the United States of America by
Cherry Lake Publishing, Ann Arbor, Michigan
www.cherrylakepublishing.com

Reading Adviser: Marla Conn, MS, Ed., Literacy specialist, Read-Ability, Inc.

Photo Credits: Cover, Zapp2Photo; page 4 (left), eHrach; Page 4 (right), Riksa Prayogi; page 6, agsandrew; page 8, Michaelpuche; page 10, Gorodenkoff; page 12, Elnur; page 14, REDPIXEL.PL; page 16, Liderina; page 18, Zapp2Photo; page 20, Zapp2Photo; page 22, Zapp2Photo; page 24, Zapp2Photo; page 26, nd3000; page 28, Lemberg Vector Studio. Source: Shutterstock.

Library of Congress Cataloging-in-Publication Data

CIP data has been filed and is available at catalog.loc.gov.

Printed in the United States of America.

Table of Contents

Hello, Emerging Tech Careers!

In the past ...

Groundbreaking inventions made life easier in many ways.

In the present ...

New technologies are changing the world in mind-boggling ways.

The future is yours to imagine!

WHAT COMES NEXT?

Who would have thought?

Alexander Graham Bell invented the first telephone in 1876. In 1879, Thomas Edison invented the first electric lightbulb. The Wright brothers successfully flew the first airplane in 1903. And don't forget Henry Ford! He invented a way to make cars quicker and cheaper.

These brilliant inventors did things that people once thought were impossible. To go from candles to electricity? From horse-drawn carriages to automobiles and airplanes? Wow!

The sky's the limit!

Now technology is being used to do even more amazing things! Take **artificial intelligence** (AI), for instance. AI involves teaching computers and other machines how to think and act in human-like ways. You may not realize it, but you probably use AI every day. Even some of your cool video games are built with artificial intelligence.

This book explores the people and professions behind artificial intelligence. Some of these careers, like machine learning engineer, are so cutting-edge that they didn't exist just a few years ago. Others, like game developer, offer exciting new twists using AI technology.

Read on to explore exciting possibilities for your future!

AI Research Scientist

Imagine a robot that can read, write, and speak just as well as any human. Or a computer that is able to teach itself new abilities and make itself more powerful. Does this sound like something from a sci-fi movie? Thanks to the latest artificial intelligence (AI) technology, it is closer to reality than you might expect.

Artificial intelligence is one of today's most exciting technological fields. It plays a role in everything from security systems to search engines. It can be used to help **diagnose** diseases or predict the weather. AI programs can even drive and park cars safely, with little or no human guidance.

AI researchers are among the top experts in their field. They are always working to push our understanding of artificial intelligence forward. They conduct experiments, collect information, and make predictions about the future of AI technology. As they learn new things, they share their ideas and findings with each other. This allows them to build on each other's research.

The term *artificial intelligence* was coined in 1955 by computer scientist John McCarthy. McCarthy organized an AI conference at New Hampshire's Dartmouth College in 1956. Some of the country's top **mathematicians** and computer scientists gathered to share their ideas about teaching computers

Imagine It!

- Find a phone, computer, or tablet with a built-in AI system. Examples include Apple's Siri, Amazon's Alexa, or Google Assistant.
- Ask the AI to do a variety of things. Make a chart to list each response.
- How often does the AI make mistakes? What do you think caused the problem? Were you requesting something too complicated? Did the AI misunderstand you?

Dig Deeper!

- Explore the history of artificial intelligence with an interactive timeline: http://www.bbc.co.uk/timelines/zq376fr.

cash machine

Thanks to artificial intelligence, ATM machines provide banking services for families like yours.

how to think for themselves. It was then that the field of AI research was born.

Early AI researchers worked hard to program computers that could do things such as solve complex math problems or play chess. These things might not seem that impressive today, but they were huge breakthroughs at the time.

In recent years, the power of AI systems has been improving at an amazing rate, and it's not showing any signs of slowing down. But the basic concepts behind this amazing technology are not new. Researchers and other innovators have been imagining intelligent machines for almost as long as computers have existed.

Today's AI researchers are working on even more exciting projects. They have created computers that can read the emotions on peoples' faces and computers that understand human speech. The future is sure to hold even more exciting discoveries in this incredible area of study.

Future AI Research Scientist

AI research is a broad and always-changing field. Even the top AI experts have to work hard to keep up with all the latest developments. Try to read as many news articles as you can about new AI technology. Even if you don't understand everything you read at first, you will keep learning more about AI and other technology over time.

Data Scientist

Even the smartest computers can't learn new things without a little help. The latest AI relies on data to become smarter. For example, if an AI computer sees enough photos of the same person, it might learn to identify that person in other photos. That is data science at work!

So, what exactly is data? Put simply, it is information that is collected to help understand something. It could be a list of statistics or a pile of photos. It could also be a list of names or the results of a poll. Politicians collect data about voters to help them decide what kinds of issues to focus on in their campaigns. Sports teams record data to help them track their players' performances.

Data also plays a huge part in creating the latest artificial intelligence programs. The most powerful AI systems are able to **analyze** huge amounts of data. They can find patterns in the data and use their findings to answer questions.

Stores might feed sales numbers into an AI system so it can figure out which products are most likely to sell well in certain locations or at certain times of the year. Doctors might present medical data from their patients to an AI system to help identify warning signs for a certain illness. The possibilities are endless as long as there is enough data for the AI to analyze.

Imagine It!

- One great way to learn about data is to follow sports.
- Pick a favorite sport and two favorite players. Use your favorite Internet search engine (like Google) to find their latest statistics.
- Make a chart comparing the two players. Which one scored the most points and made the least mistakes?

Dig Deeper!

- Watch a video to learn about the different kinds of problems people can solve using data science: http://bit.ly/MicrosoftDataSci.
- Check out this website for a collection of interesting data about people in the United States: https://www.census.gov/schools/facts.

Data analysts work with big data.

Data scientists are data experts. They know which kinds of information can be used to find out the answers to different types of questions. They can figure out the best way to collect large amounts of data. They are also able to organize and present the data in a way that makes sense and is easy to understand.

Importantly, data scientists also know how to work with data after it has been collected and organized. Sometimes data can be misleading if you don't know what to look for. Data scientists are trained to avoid drawing the wrong conclusions from the information they collect. This helps them ensure that the right kinds of data are used to teach AI systems new things. It also allows them to notice when the AI is doing something the wrong way.

Future Data Scientist

Are you interested in a career in the rapidly growing field of data science? You'll probably need a college degree in a subject such as math, computer science, or engineering. Some colleges even offer specialized data science degrees. Before heading to college, you'll want to study subjects such as statistics and computer programming.

Game Developer

You are enjoying your new video game, but you can't believe how challenging it is. The computer-controlled enemies behave just like human players. They seem to know all the best tricks and when to use them. When you try new strategies, the enemies even adjust their behavior in response.

Today's video games often feature computer-controlled **opponents** that behave with surprising realism. The challenge of trying to defeat these skilled enemies can make a game a lot of fun. And this fascinating feature is all thanks to the power of AI.

Believe it or not, playing games was one of the first things AI systems learned to do. In 1951, researcher Christopher Strachey created a computer program that could play checkers. This was a huge breakthrough at the time. By the 1960s, computers were skillfully playing chess, a much more complex game.

The earliest video games, which were created in the 1960s, required two human players to compete against each other. But by the 1970s, game developers were adding single-player modes where players could compete against AI opponents. As games became more complex over time, so did the AI powering these computer opponents.

Imagine It!

- Play a game against a friend. It can be a video game or a board game.
- What kind of strategies does your friend use? What kind of mistakes does he or she make?
- Make a list of the traits an AI system would need to mimic your friend's play style.

Dig Deeper!

- Learn to code simple AI programs for *Minecraft* characters to follow: https://code.org/minecraft.
- Once you've mastered that game, try other programming lessons at Code.org: https://code.org/learn.

Game developers use artificial intelligence to create popular games played on smartphones and tablets.

AI in video games is different than the types of AI used for real-world tasks. A game can be programmed to give the AI enemy information that a human player would not have access to in real life. For example, an enemy in an action game does not need to truly "see" your character to find you and attack. Instead, the game can simply tell the AI where you are. Real-world applications of AI do not get to take these kinds of shortcuts.

Because AI-controlled players in a video game can "cheat" in this way, game developers face a unique challenge. They want to create opponents that are challenging to defeat. However, they do not want the game to seem unfair to human players. After all, that wouldn't be very fun!

People who program AI for video games have a very different set of skills and talents from those who create other kinds of AI systems. But if you're interested in both games and AI, it could be the perfect career for you!

Future Game Developers

If you want to help create AI for games, you'll need programming skills and a college degree in a field such as computer science. In the meantime, try to become an expert in what makes games fun to play. Any time you play a game, think carefully about which parts are good and which are bad. Try brainstorming ways to improve the game.

Machine Learning Engineer

Have you ever started typing something into a **search engine**, only to see the computer automatically fill in the rest of what you wanted to type? How did it know what you wanted to search for? Is the computer reading your mind? Not at all! It has simply learned what kinds of things you like to do online.

Every time you search for something online, the search engine keeps track of what you look for and what you click on. It also keeps track of the same data for millions of other people around the world. Using all of this information, the search engine can do a pretty good job of predicting what most people want to search for.

This process is an example of something called machine learning. Machine learning is an area of artificial intelligence focused on creating computer programs that can learn new things and develop new skills.

There are three main steps to the machine learning process. First, data needs to be collected. In the example above, the data is all of the web searching done by people around the world. The second step is called training. Here, the AI looks at all of the data to find patterns. Finally, the third step is for the AI to create a model. The model is a set of rules and processes based on these patterns. For example,

Imagine It!

- Imagine you are a machine learning engineer working on a project that will teach a computer to give people movie recommendations. Sketch out answers to these questions:
- What kinds of information will the computer need to make an accurate prediction?
- How could you collect this information to train the computer?
- Is there any way to keep the computer from recommending movies people have already seen?

Dig Deeper!

- Check out this video from Google to learn more about the basics of machine learning: http://bit.ly/GoogleMachLearn.

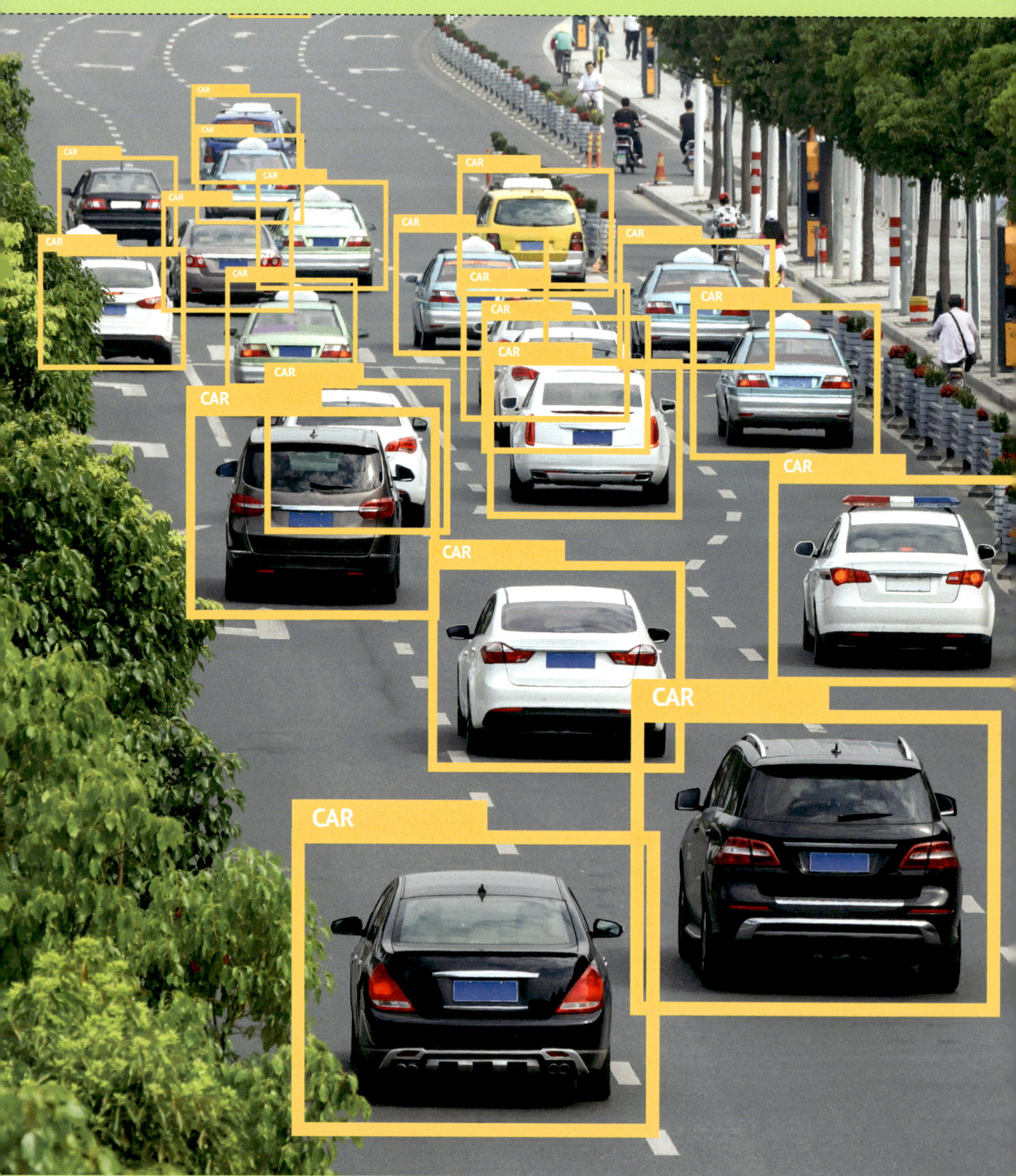

Car recognition software is one way that machine learning is used.

let's say the AI has collected data from millions of searches that begin with "what is ...". Now it will develop a model for filling in likely ways that people will want to finish that phrase.

Machine learning can be applied in many useful ways. It helps decide which video to show you next on YouTube. It knows how to filter useless spam messages out of your email inbox. It is even used to improve **self-driving cars**, airplane autopilot systems, and the voice recognition software used in phones and tablets.

The people who work with machine learning systems are called machine learning engineers. These people think up new ways to use machine learning. They also collect data, create the programs needed to train the AI, and test the resulting models to make sure they are useful and accurate.

Future Machine Learning Engineer

Machine learning is a very popular area of AI research today. If you can become an expert in this field, you'll have no trouble finding a good job. To prepare, start learning how to program computers. You should also try to keep up with news about breakthroughs in machine learning. Reading about someone else's discovery might give you an idea no one else has thought of!

Robotics Engineer

Can you imagine if your doctor was a **robot**? Or if your school had robot teachers? While neither of these things is likely to happen tomorrow, they could be coming sooner than you'd think. Thanks to powerful AI, robots could one day be able to do many jobs that once required human workers.

Robots are already all around us. These **automated** machines work in factories, assembling everything from cars to computers. They are in our homes, working as vacuum cleaners and lawn mowers. Some stores and businesses are even starting to use robots to greet people and talk to customers.

Robots rely on computers to make them work. The computers are programmed to tell the robots how to act in different situations. For example, a robotic arm in a factory might be programmed to perform the same simple job over and over again as cars move down an assembly line. But a **humanoid** robot built to talk with people would have much more complex programming based on cutting-edge AI technology.

Artificial intelligence will make tomorrow's robots smarter than ever before. Talented robotics engineers are always hard at work building robots that take advantage of the latest advances in AI. These workers

Imagine It!

- Imagine you're an engineer who's just learned about a huge new development in AI facial recognition.
- What kind of robot could you make using this kind of AI?
- Sketch out what you think the robot might look like. Label the robot's parts.

Dig Deeper!

- Watch a video to see how AI helps a robot move around on two legs and use its arms like a human: http://bit.ly/WSJRobot.

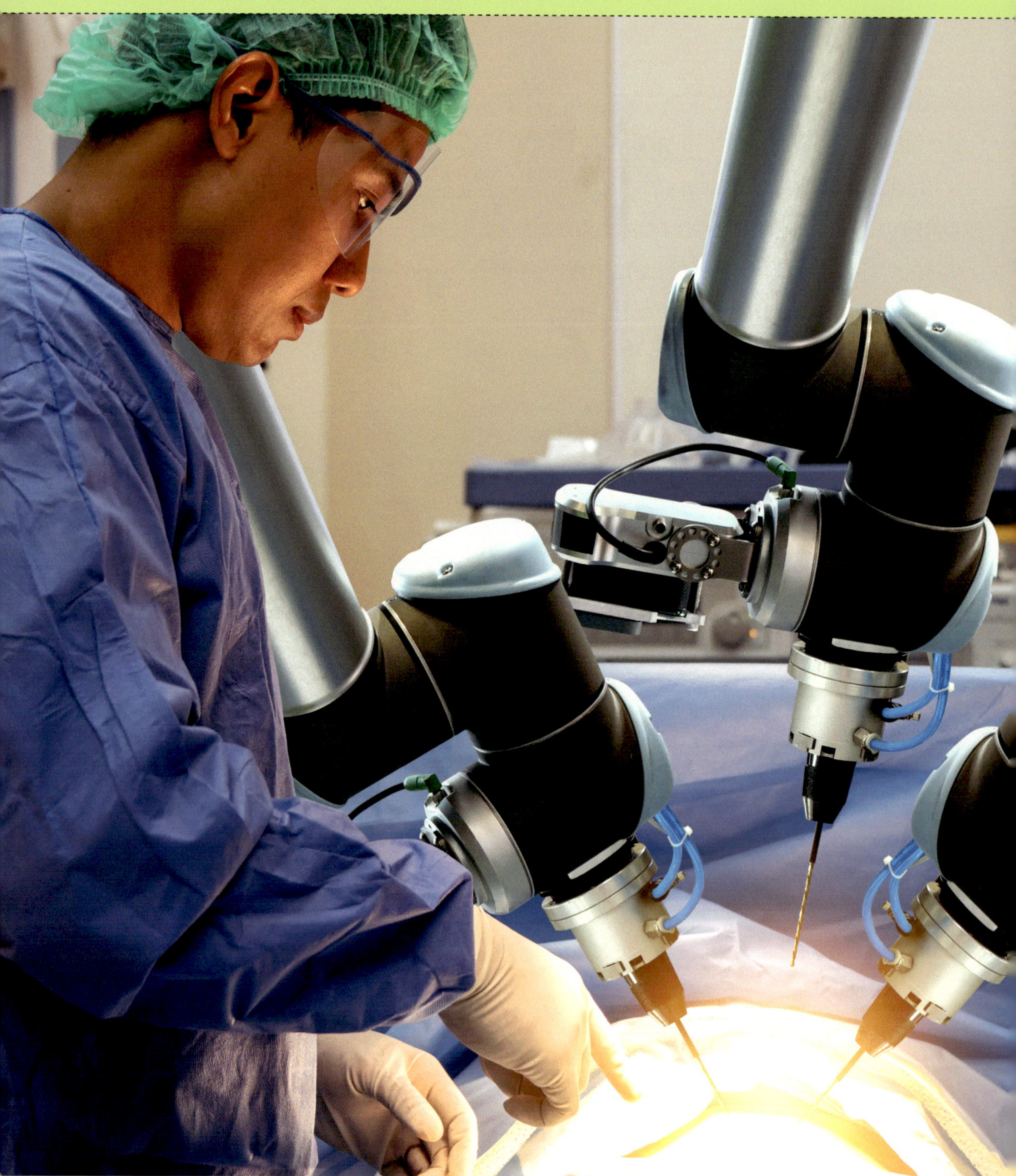

Robotic medical equipment help doctors perform life-saving surgeries.

use the knowledge gained by AI scientists, machine learning engineers, and other AI experts to create new kinds of robots and improve old ones.

For example, AI researchers have discovered a method for computers to determine which emotions a person is feeling by scanning the person's facial expression. Robotics engineers might integrate this technology into a robot that helps customers in stores. The robot would be able to tell if customers are happy with its service just by looking at their faces.

Many of the incredible new robots you hear about in the news are **prototypes**. This means they are early versions. As incredible as they are, they might have flaws that prevent them from working correctly in real life. A big part of an engineer's job is to continually improve their prototypes and solve problems that arise. This process can take a long time, but the results can be truly spectacular.

Future Robotics Engineer

You can start learning the skills robotics engineers use every day long before heading off to college to study engineering. Try creating your own robots using systems such as Lego Mindstorms (https://www.lego.com/en-us/mindstorms). Practice building and programming robots to make your everyday chores easier. Start simple, then keep working your way up to tougher challenges!

Software Developer

Have you ever been frustrated with a computer program or a website? Maybe you can't figure out how to use a major feature. Or maybe you just don't like the way the program works. If you've ever found yourself thinking of ways to improve an **app**, you might be a natural-born software developer!

Many of the apps you use on smartphones and tablets rely on AI to work correctly. So do a lot of the most popular websites, such as Google and Facebook. However, there is more to these apps and sites than just the AI itself. Skilled software developers have to create programs to turn powerful AI technology into something people can use in their everyday lives.

For example, AI researchers might come up with a new way for computers to figure out which kinds of news articles different people like to read. By itself, this AI isn't much good to the average person. But if it was built into an app that collected news stories from around the web for people to read, it could be really helpful.

It often takes a team of developers to design and build the apps and websites that bring the benefits of AI to people around the world. A project might start with developers listing features they would like to include in their program.

Imagine It!

- Make a list of your five most-used apps or websites. Examples might include YouTube, Amazon, or Google.
- Search online to find out how AI is used in these programs or sites. Are you surprised at the answers?
- Now that you know how AI affects these programs, can you predict how it might be used to improve them in the future?

Dig Deeper!

- Check out some apps created by a young software developer at www.madebyyuma.com. He also makes YouTube videos to teach other kids about coding.

Software developers use artificial intelligence to create useful programs and apps.

Once the team has some ideas in mind, some of the members might focus on developing the look and feel of a program. They figure out the best way to arrange information on a screen. They also come up with interesting, easy-to-use ways of controlling a program.

Other developers might work almost entirely on the coding that goes into making the program's features work correctly. Their work could determine how quickly the program loads and responds when a user inputs a command. It could also determine other important behind-the-scenes aspects of the program.

As the project starts to come together, it is time to test for bugs. The development team tries to use the program in every possible way they can think of. This helps them find programming errors or see if one of their planned features isn't working as well as they had hoped. They can then make changes to fix the problems.

Future Software Developer

The number one skill you'll need if you want to become a successful software developer is the ability to program computers. Teach yourself to code or take programming classes if you can. Once you have the basics down, start designing and building your own programs and apps. Think of something you'd like your computer or phone to do, and make it happen!

Can You Imagine?

Innovation always starts with an idea. This was true for Alexander Graham Bell, Thomas Edison, Henry Ford, and the Wright brothers. It is still true today as innovators imagine new ways to use artificial intelligence. And it will still be true in the future when you begin your high-tech career. So ...

What is your big idea?

Think of a cool new way to use artificial intelligence. Write a story or draw a picture to share your idea with others.

Please do **NOT** write in this book if it doesn't belong to you.
Gather your own paper and art supplies and get creative with your ideas!

Glossary

analyze (AN-uh-lize) to discover or reveal something through detailed examination

app (AHP) a computer program that is written and designed for a specific purpose on a smartphone or tablet

artificial intelligence (ahr-tuh-FISH-uhl in-TEL-ih-juhns) the ability of a digital computer or computer-controlled robot to perform tasks commonly associated with humans

automated (AW-tuh-may-ted) operated without direct control, such as machines doing the job of humans

breakthroughs (BRAYK-throoz) successful, often sudden developments that make progress possible

diagnose (dye-uhg-NOHS) identify the nature of an illness or other problem by examination of the symptoms

humanoid (HYOO-muh-noyd) something that has an appearance resembling a human without actually being one

innovations (in-uh-VAY-shuhnz) new ideas or inventions

mathematicians (math-uh-muh-TISH-uhnz) experts in mathematics, or the study of numbers, quantities, shapes, and measurements and how they relate to one another

opponents (uh-POH-nuhnts) people who take an opposite position in a debate, contest, or conflict

prototypes (PROH-tuh-tipes) the first versions of inventions that test an idea to see it if will work

robot (ROH-baht) machines that are programmed to perform complex human tasks

search engine (SURCH EN-jin) a website or software that searches the Internet for documents that contain a keyword, phrase, or subject that is requested by the user

self-driving cars (SELF-DRIVE-ing KAHRZ) robotic vehicles designed to travel between destinations without human operators

Index

About the Author

Joshua Gregory is the author of more than 125 books for young readers. He currently lives in Chicago, Illinois.